Zeus and the
Thunderbolt of Doom

HEROES IN TRAINING

Zeus and the Thunderbolt of Doom

Joan Holub and
Suzanne Williams

SCHOLASTIC INC.

ISBN 978-0-545-55937-9

Text copyright © 2012 by Joan Holub and Suzanne Williams.
Illustrations copyright © 2012 by Craig Phillips.
All rights reserved. Published by Scholastic Inc.,
557 Broadway, New York, NY 10012,
by arrangement with Aladdin Paperbacks, an imprint of
Simon & Schuster Children's Publishing Division.
SCHOLASTIC and associated logos are trademarks
and/or registered trademarks of Scholastic Inc.

12 11 10 9 8 7 6 5 4 3 2 1   13 14 15 16 17 18/0

Printed in the U.S.A.   40

First Scholastic printing, January 2013

Designed by Karin Paprocki
The text of this book was set in Adobe Garamond.

⚡ Contents ⚡

Greetings, Mortal Readers,

I am Pythia, the Oracle of Delphi, in Greece. I have the power to see the future. Hear my prophecy:

Ahead I see dancers lurking. Wait—make that *danger* lurking. (The future can be blurry, especially when my eyeglasses are foggy.)

Anyhoo, beware! Titan giants now rule all of Earth's domains—oceans, mountains, forests, and the depths of the Underwear. Oops—make that *Underworld*. Led by King Cronus, they are out to destroy us all!

Yet I foresee hope. A band of rightful rulers called Olympians will arise. Though their size and youth are no match for the Titans, they will be giant in heart, mind, and spirit. They await their leader—a very special, yet clueless godboy. One who is destined to become king of the gods and ruler of the heavens.

If he is brave enough.

For saving the world will not be greasy. Um—*easy.*

Prologue

OVER THE TEETH AND PAST THE GUMS, look out, belly, here Zeus comes!" King Cronus, the big bad king of the Titan giants, tossed up the object he held. It flew high above his head. As it arced downward, he caught it in his mouth. Then he swallowed. *GULP!*

Far below, five Olympian childgods were being held captive deep inside his dark, giant belly. They heard squishy sounds. Something

came whooshing down the Titan king's throat like a snowball rolling down Mount Olympus. They all pressed back to avoid being squished by whatever was coming.

Splat! The new arrival hit the bottom of Cronus's stomach.

"Hello?" Poseidon whispered into the darkness. "Are you one of us? Another Olympian?"

No answer.

"Maybe he's dead," Hades said in a gloomy voice.

Just then Cronus burped big. As his mouth opened, light speared down his throat into his belly. The young childgods gasped.

"That's no Olympian. It's a stone!" Demeter exclaimed.

Hera ran her hand over the smooth cone-shaped stone. It was half as tall as she was. "This thing could be our ticket out of here!" she whispered in excitement. Feeling around, she found a sharp fish bone left over from Cronus's supper last night. She began to blindly scratch a message on the stone: *Help us! We are in Cronus.*

"Wait a sec," Hades said when she told them what she'd written. "I'm not sure I want to leave. I mean, Cronus swallowed us as babies, and we haven't been outside since. Who knows what dangers might be lurking out there? Besides, I like it in here." For whatever reason, gloomy, smelly places didn't bother him.

"Then stay if you want to," said Hestia. "But the rest of us want *out*!"

Poseidon nodded. "Yeah. Do you want to be trapped in here forever? If we don't get out, we'll never age past ten. Cronus's magic spell won't let us."

Before Hades could answer, they heard Cronus bark out an order to his army. He was riding into battle in the town of Delphi. Soon they heard the clank of swords all around them. There were more shouts—and screams, too.

The Olympians quickly made a slingshot out of an old Minotaur wishbone and a strip of elastic sinew. (There was all kinds of gross stuff lying around in Cronus's belly.) After they set the inscribed stone into the slingshot, they pulled it back tight.

On the count of three, they let it go. *Boing!* The cone-shaped stone shot up Cronus's throat and burst out of his mouth. The fact that it knocked out one of his front teeth as it exited was just icing on the cake.

Although they had no way of knowing it, the stone hit the ground rolling. It skittered and bumped its way down a hillside. Then it came to rest at the bottom of a set of marble steps that led up to a temple.

Immediately a white-robed woman wearing eyeglasses hurried down the steps to pick it up. It was almost as if she'd been expecting the stone to arrive! Hugging it to her chest, she disappeared into the temple with it.

CHAPTER ONE

Ten Years Later

FLASH! LIGHTNING ZIGZAGGED DOWN from the sky.

Crack! It struck a hundred-year-old oak tree and split it in half. A tremendous clap of thunder boomed overhead.

"Yikes!" shouted ten-year-old Zeus. He dropped the wooden sword he'd been practicing with. Leaping out of the way of the falling tree trunk, he took off running. He had a feeling the next bolt would be aimed at him. Why? Because he'd been struck by lightning dozens of times already in his short life.

A wild wind whipped through his dark hair as he raced for safety. With his heart beating faster than a hummingbird's wings, Zeus dove through the entrance of a cave. A new lightning bolt struck the dirt just outside it, barely missing his foot.

Flash! Boom! The storm raged all around him as he cowered behind a boulder. This cave was his home—the only one he'd ever known. And as far back as he can remember, thunderstorms had been a daily event here in Crete.

He was terrified of them. Who wanted to be hit by lightning after all? It tossed you into the air and rattled your brain. He ought to know!

But that wasn't the scariest part. Each time he'd been struck, he'd heard a voice murmuring to him, *"You are the one."* What could it mean?

Another flash of lightning sliced through the clouds, followed by rumbling thunder. Rain lashed the ground. It flattened the grasses in front of the cave and churned the dirt to mud. But then, as suddenly as it had begun, the thunderstorm moved off. Clouds lifted, the sun came out, and the earth began to dry again.

Feeling braver now, Zeus stuck his thumbs in his ears and wiggled his fingers. "Nyah, nyah, you missed me," he taunted toward the sound of distant thunder.

Nearby he heard the clanking sound of a bell followed by a bleat. *Maa!* A goat trotted into view. "Amalthea!" He threw his arms around the goat's neck, glad to see her unharmed.

Moments later a nymph slipped free of a slender willow tree and scampered over to milk the goat. When she finished, she wordlessly handed Zeus a rich, creamy cup of milk. He drank it down in a single gulp, then nodded to her in thanks.

Stomp! Stomp! Stomp! The ground beneath them began to shake. It sounded like a whole army was heading their way. The nymph's eyes went wide.

"Hide!" Zeus hissed. He fled to the cave again while she leaped into the willow. Merging with its trunk and branches, she went invisible. Peeking out from behind the boulder, Zeus was relieved to see that Amalthea was nowhere in sight. He hoped she would stay away until this new danger passed.

Before long, three men marched into the clearing. Half-giants, by the look of them. They were so tall that their heads were even with the top of the nymph's willow. Yet they weren't as tall as a true Titan giant. True giants stood as tall as oaks!

These half-giants wore polished helmets and carried spears. Two letters were carved on their iron helmets and armor: *KC*. Which stood for "King Cronus." Which meant they were Cronies—soldiers working for the Titan king.

Zeus shuddered. Cronies terrorized the countryside, stealing money and food from farmers and villagers. Anyone who resisted was dragged off to a dungeon—or worse. He cringed lower in his hiding place.

One of the half-giants, a Crony with a double chin, scratched his big round belly. He gazed down the mountainside. "Lots of apple orchards down there," he said. "Should be easy pickings."

A black-bearded Crony laughed. "Especially since we can force the farmers to do the picking *for* us!"

Zeus trembled with anger. Half of him was ready to tell those half-giants off. But the other half was too chicken. Besides, what could he do? He was only a kid. They'd crush him like a bug under their humongous sandals!

He'd heard tales of others who'd tried to fight and had failed. Now everyone pretty much bowed down to the Cronies. It beat getting stomped.

Maa! Maa! Suddenly he heard the faint ringing of Amalthea's bell again. Oh no! She was coming back.

As the clinking grew louder, the Cronies spotted her. "Mmm. I fancy goat meat for supper," the double-chinned one said. He drew back his spear. Zeus opened his mouth to yell, *Stop!* But before he could, the half-giant dropped his weapon.

"Yeowch!" Double Chin yelped, slapping the back of his neck. Meanwhile, Amalthea trotted downhill again, out of reach.

The other two Cronies frowned at him. "What's with you?" Blackbeard asked.

"I got stung by a bee!" Double Chin grumped.

Zeus grinned as he watched the bee buzz around the half-giant's head and then fly off. It was Melissa.

Ever since he'd mysteriously arrived at the cave as an orphaned baby ten years ago, she had kept watch over him along with the nymph and Amalthea. He was glad for their companionship. Still, he did often wonder who his parents were and why they'd abandoned him.

The third half-giant, who sported a huge tattoo of a lion on his shoulder, looked around nervously. "We should go," he said. "In case there are more bees."

Zeus almost laughed aloud to think of King Cronus's fearsome soldiers being afraid of something as small as a bee. Normally Melissa wouldn't even hurt a fly. But cruel half-giants deserved whatever she could dish out.

"What's that?" Double Chin asked, staring toward the cave. Zeus shivered. Had he been spotted? If so, he was doomed! But then he realized what the Crony was really staring at— Zeus's drinking cup. He'd left it on the ground in full view!

Lion Tattoo was first to reach the cup. Picking it up, he sniffed it curiously. Then he held it upside down over the palm of one hand. "Fresh milk," he grunted as a few white drops trickled out. "Someone's here."

All three Cronies looked toward the entrance to the cave. Ducking his head, Zeus tucked himself small. If only he could merge into the boulder like the nymph had merged with the tree.

Footsteps pounded closer. Hot breath. Suddenly Zeus was plucked from his hiding place like a weed from a garden. His legs dangled helplessly in the air and his arms spun.

Holding him by two fat fingers, Double Chin stared at him, eye-to-eye, licking his chops. Zeus squeezed his eyes shut, as if doing so might make the half-giants disappear. Didn't work. And it didn't drown out the terrible sound of Double Chin's next words either.

"Fee, fi, fo, fun. I smell boy. Gonna eat me one!"

CHAPTER TWO

Good-bye, Crete!

PLEASE DON'T EAT ME! I'M PRETTY SURE I taste icky. Like . . . like cave scum or bat poop," Zeus croaked out. "And I'm bony. I might get stuck in your throat."

Double Chin laughed. "Ha! Grease you up with a little garlic oil and I could swallow you whole, easy as pie!"

"Yum, pie." Blackbeard sighed longingly, like he was remembering pies he'd enjoyed in the past.

"Or we could take you to King Cronus and *he* could swallow you whole!" Lion Tattoo said. He winked at his pals. "The boy would have plenty of company down in the king's belly."

What's that supposed to mean? Zeus wondered. He thought about trying to wrench himself free from Double Chin's grasp. But the ground was a long way down.

"How should we fix him?" Double Chin asked the other two. "Grilled?"

"I vote mashed," said Blackbeard.

"Later," said Lion Tattoo. "Lunch will have to wait. We need to hit the road."

He must be the leader of the three, thought Zeus.

Double Chin set Zeus on the ground. Then he quickly whipped off his KC helmet. Bending down, he took it in both hands and stuffed it over Zeus's head. It was so big that it slid all the way down over his shoulders to his wrists.

Stunned, Zeus stared out between the bars of the grill in the front of the iron helmet. He was trapped in helmet jail!

He couldn't move his arms at all. The helmet was so tight, it pinned them to his sides. He tried running away but tripped and couldn't get up again. He rolled around on the ground like a bug on its back, unable to right himself.

Double Chin and Blackbeard shook with laughter. But Lion Tattoo roared, "Move it!"

Instantly Double Chin set Zeus on his feet again. Then he poked the helmet with the tip of his spear. "You heard him. Move it!"

Zeus moved it. What else could he do?

As they started down the hillside, something swooped down at them. The nymph had flown out of the willow. She was trying to save him! But the half-giants brushed her aside as if she weighed less than a leaf.

They'd gone only a few more steps when Amalthea appeared. The goat charged after them. When she caught up to Blackbeard, she leaped up and butted his behind.

"Why, you—" he yelled. Whirling around, he grabbed the goat around the neck.

"No!" Zeus gasped, sure that Amalthea was a goner. Suddenly he heard a buzzing sound above him. *Melissa!* She made a beeline for the half-giants.

Zeus cheered. "You go, bee!"

"Get away!" screeched Lion Tattoo, waving his hands in the air to fight her off.

Double Chin reached out and backhanded the bee hard enough to send her tumbling into a bed of daisies. Zeus was relieved to see Melissa crawl under a toadstool, unharmed.

Meanwhile, the wriggling goat slipped from Blackbeard's big hands and ran off. Blackbeard took a few steps after her. But when she zig-zagged to the top of a cliff, he gave up.

"Guess that goat got your goat, huh?" Zeus teased him. "Guess I'm too much trouble to keep around. Maybe you should let me go."

Blackbeard just glared at him.

"Not a chance," said Lion Tattoo, starting off again. "Little snacks like you eventually grow up into fighting men. Who knows what trouble you could cause us then?"

"Who? Me?" Zeus tried not to trip over his feet as he hurried to keep up with the giants. He was a ten-year-old boy. An orphan who lived in a cave. Although he liked to pretend to sword fight, he had no real skills. His parents, whoever they were, hadn't stuck around to teach him any. And though he longed to see the world, he'd never traveled anywhere. What possible trouble could he cause? He was a nobody!

Zeus forced out a giggle as he stumbled along. "Oh, ha-ha, hee-hee," he said. "I get it. You were joking, right? 'Cause there's no way you could be scared of me. That would be like being afraid of something as tiny as—" Cocking his head to one side, he pretended to think for a second. Then, brightening up, he glanced at Lion Tattoo through the grill: "—as tiny as a *bee*!"

The other two Cronies snickered. Lion Tattoo scowled. "As soon as we find some garlic oil, you are toast!" he told Zeus.

Blackbeard's stomach growled, and he eyed Zeus longingly. "Yum—toast."

Uh-oh! He'd better not act *too* annoying, Zeus decided. Because his captors might decide to eat him right now!

"Don't listen to them. I like you, kid," Double Chin said. "You've got spunk."

Zeus wasn't sure what "spunk" was. But he

hoped it wasn't something half-giants found tasty. "Does that mean you'll let me go?"

"Naw." Double Chin shook his head. "You're coming with us. We could use a little entertainment."

"Yeah, let's see how fast he can run," Lion Tattoo said with a sinister smile. With that, the half-giants went crashing down the mountainside. Because they'd made him march ahead of them, Zeus had to scramble to keep from being trampled. Tripping, he fell onto his side and rolled downhill.

Thunk! He came to a stop when he crashed into a tree trunk in the apple orchard. Luckily, the helmet protected him from harm. As he dizzily rose to his feet and staggered on, the three Cronies entered the orchard too.

They began uprooting trees with their bare hands. Stripping the apples from the branches as if they were grapes on a vine, they tossed them into their mouths. They stomped downhill, chomping and crunching. Whenever Zeus slowed, they prodded him with their spears to make him keep up.

At last they reached the sea. Zeus hadn't seen a single person the whole way downhill. Everyone must've heard the Cronies coming. They weren't exactly quiet. And having heard them, anyone with an ounce of smarts would be hiding.

"Look!" bellowed Double Chin, pointing to a ship tied up to a dock. "Free transport."

The ship's sails were half unfurled as if its crew had quickly abandoned ship. The Cronies tossed Zeus on board, jumped in, and set sail.

"Wait!" Zeus yelled. "Where are we going?"

CHAPTER THREE

Trouble Ahoy!

NEVER YOU MIND WHERE WE'RE HEADED, Snackboy!" Lion Tattoo growled in answer to Zeus's question.

Maybe he was still feeling touchy about everyone laughing at his fear of bees. Still, knowing that this half-giant leader was afraid of something so small made Zeus feel less embarrassed about his own fear of thunderstorms.

"We're heading for the Mediterranean Sea.

Going all the way to Delphi," Double Chin told him.

"Delphi, *Greece*?" Zeus asked, astonished.

"No—Delphi on the moon," joked Blackbeard. "Of course Delphi, Greece. Gonna join up with Cronus's army there. And it'll be a long, *hungry* trip," he added pointedly.

Argh! That didn't sound good. Still, Zeus couldn't help feeling a little excited. His cave in Crete had been so boring. (Except for the thunderstorms!) He was grateful to the nymph, bee, and goat for taking good care of him there. But deep down, he'd always believed he was destined for a life that was more awesome.

For years he'd thought his parents would come back to get him one day. But over time that dream had faded. Now that he was off to see the world, maybe he'd find *them*. If he didn't become snack food first!

"What are you going to do in Greece?" he asked.

Blackbeard grinned evilly, patting his belly. "Bake us some boy pie, first thing."

Zeus thought it best not to reply to that. As the half-giants guided the ship, he watched it cut through the sparkling blue waters of the Mediterranean Sea. He'd always longed for adventure. This would have been a fine one if he'd been with different, less hungry companions.

Seeming to sense his fear, Double Chin tried to reassure him. "Aw, just ignore him, Snack. We're all full of apples for now. Don't worry. You got hours to live."

He was nicer than the other two, Zeus decided. Sort of.

Suddenly the wind began to whip up. "Storm's on the way," Lion Tattoo noted, eyeing the darkening sky.

He was right, Zeus realized as he stared at the swirling black clouds overhead. This morning's thunderstorm was coming back. And now there was nowhere to run! Stuck in the middle of the sea, he'd be an easy target for the lightning bolts that seem to chase him wherever he went.

He tried not to panic. But as he heard thunder growl in the distance, he wondered how these half-giants might like him fried. By lightning.

The soldiers got busy adjusting the sails. The billowing wind filled them, pushing the ship along at a fast clip. Zeus stared out between the bars of his helmet jail, his eyes wild.

"See that storm? It's after me," he told the half-giants. "And if lightning strikes this ship, I won't be the only one to fry." When his captors didn't reply, Zeus hopped up and down. "Are you listening, you Cronies? You should sail back to Crete and let me go!"

Blackbeard reached out and whacked the side of Zeus's helmet. "Don't call us that! We hate that nickname. We're half-giants, got it?"

"Well, my name's not Snack either!" Zeus yelled, feeling grumpy himself. "It's Zeus."

At that, Lion Tattoo's head whipped around to stare at him. "Zeus? Hmm. Why does that name ring a bell?"

Zeus shrugged. When he'd been abandoned as a baby, the nymph had found him lying in a basket with a scroll tucked beside him. One word had been written on it: *Zeus.* That was all. No way this half-giant could possibly have heard of him.

"Incoming!" Double Chin shouted, drawing everyone's attention. He was pointing at the sky again.

In the faraway clouds Zeus saw five dark blobs soaring toward them. Whatever they were, the half-giants seemed worried about them.

Barely a second later the storm was upon them, lashing them with rain and wind. Waves rocked them to and fro, tossing the ship around like a toy. His three captors had all they could do to control the ship.

Thunder rumbled, closer now. "Here we go again," Zeus muttered.

But for some reason the lightning didn't strike him. And instead of trying to sink them, the wind was pushing them in the direction they wanted to go. At this speedy rate they would reach Delphi in no time. It was almost as if the storm wanted to hurry them along.

Caw! Caw! Zeus looked upward again. Those five black blobs had gained on them. They were birds! Big ones.

"Aghhh!" The half-giants scurried around in frantic circles on deck, darting alarmed looks at them.

"Some soldiers you are—scared of crows!" Zeus shouted over the wind.

"Those are Harpies, you idiot!" Double Chin yelled back. "They'll peck your eyes out in two seconds."

Zeus stuck his nose through the bars of his helmet jail and stared harder at the birds overhead. Whoa! They were bigger than he was, he realized. And they had long curly hair that blew out behind them as they dipped and rose on currents of air. Birds with *hair*?

Then he noticed something even weirder. They had women's faces! But what had him *really* shaking in his sandals was the sight of their curved, razor-sharp beaks. That, and the demented look in their beady eyes. He shuddered.

Quickly he gathered his courage. Those lady birds might be vicious, but they were also a distraction. And while the Cronies' attention was on them, he might just be able to hide. But where?

CHAPTER FOUR

Harpies

TRYING TO KEEP HIS BALANCE ON THE bobbing ship, Zeus walked the deck searching for a hiding place. Any hiding place.

Just then the ship rolled hard to one side. He stumbled and tripped over the railing. Then he was falling. Tumbling overboard!

Splash! He hit the stormy sea headfirst, plunging deep. When he bobbed upright again, he coughed and sucked air back into his lungs. Stunned, Zeus watched the ship sail away.

He treaded water, kicking his legs hard. He didn't want to drown out here!

But with his shoulders trapped inside Double Chin's helmet, he had no chance of saving himself. The iron helmet was heavy. Sure, he could swim, but not without the use of his arms. Especially not in these wild seas. And he was pretty far from land.

"Help!" he yelled toward the ship.

To his surprise, it turned around and came toward him, tacking back and forth into the wind. Lion Tattoo was at the helm, looking oddly determined to rescue him. Why were they coming back? Were those apples wearing off? Were they hungry again?

When the ship got closer, Lion Tattoo pointed a finger at Zeus. "You! I just remembered where

I heard your name." He leaned over the side, trying to snag Zeus's helmet's grill with the hook on the end of his long harpoon.

Zeus frowned and backpedaled his legs. How could the half-giant have heard of him?

If Lion Tattoo really did know something about him, maybe he knew who his parents were. Zeus had been unable to learn anything about them over the years. But now hope rose in him again that he might discover something.

Just as the harpoon's hook drew near, a shadow fell over him. *Caw! Caw!* Zeus looked up. The Harpies!

Whoosh! One of them dove straight at him. Her dagger-sharp claws wrapped tight around the helmet's grill. Zeus ducked his head as far back inside the helmet as he could.

At the same time, Lion Tattoo swung his harpoon wildly. But all he caught was dead air.

Because Zeus was already in the clutches of the boy-pecking Harpies!

Up and up he went. Higher and higher. Then he was flying. Where were the Harpies taking him? Probably to their nest, where he would become Harpy bird-baby food. It seemed like all anyone wanted to do today was eat him!

Zeus wiggled around, trying to escape from the helmet. It began to loosen. He gave a hard bounce. Then he was free!

And falling!

Before he dropped far, claws wrapped around each of his arms and held him fast. Two other Harpies had grabbed him, one on either side. At least he was out of helmet jail now, though this wasn't much better.

"Where are you taking me?" he demanded. But his words were whipped away by the wind.

And so they flew onward, the ship swiftly becoming a mere speck in the distance.

He hadn't wanted to be the half-giants' snack. But he didn't want to be pecked to death by these bird-women or their babies either. All of a sudden, getting swallowed whole by Blackbeard seemed like the lesser of two evils.

Turning his head, Zeus stared at the far horizon. He could no longer see the ship or his home on the island of Crete. Was he never to see his friends again—the nymph, bee, and goat, who'd raised him for ten years? He'd wanted to see the world, but not *this* way! For now he was at the mercy of these crazy birds. And he could only wait and see what they would do.

Caw! Caw!

Heading north for Greece, the Harpies flew like the wind, staying just ahead of the storm. The firebirds formed a V shape, with one bird in the lead and two behind on either side. Every so often they changed places, as the lead lady bird tired.

Hoo-loob! Hoo-loob! Zeus turned his head and saw that a pigeon was now flying alongside them. A rolled-up piece of papyrus was clamped in its beak. A message! He could read only two words of it: *Capture Zeus.*

Huh? Zeus blinked his eyes a few times. Was his vision playing tricks on him? Maybe the high altitude was affecting his brain, causing him to see things that couldn't possibly be.

Less than an hour later the Harpies reached the shore of Greece. Far below them the harbor was full of ships. The pigeon dove, heading for one of them. They were military ships, Zeus realized. With dozens of half-giants on board.

He watched the pigeon deliver its message to a half-giant in a captain's uniform. After quickly scanning it, the captain pointed up at the Harpies. He shouted orders to his crew.

To Zeus's amazement, everyone began running around. They were giving chase. But there was no way these Cronies could catch them. They were on the ground. He and the Harpies were flying.

Why was the army after him, anyway? Were they hungry too, like the half-giants he'd met before? Surely there were other boys they could eat. Boys who'd be easier to catch!

The Harpies flew on, past hillsides covered with grapevines and olive trees. Now and then, Zeus saw a battalion of the king's Cronies marching in formation in the countryside. *Why so many?* he wondered. It almost looked like they were preparing for war!

CHAPTER FIVE

Bolt

I T WASN'T LONG BEFORE ZEUS SPIED A city below. Marble buildings with tall, white Ionic columns and smaller stone houses clung to a hillside. His winged captors dipped lower, going in for a landing.

Zeus's sandals touched down. He hit the ground running. Then he tripped and rolled in a series of head-over-heels somersaults.

When he finally came to a stop, he sat up

on the dirt road, feeling dizzy. The five Harpies stood in a ring around him. He didn't see any nests nearby. Or any hungry baby birds. *Good.* But what did these Harpies want?

The biggest of them stared at him and licked her pointy beak lips. The others had black eyes, but this one's eyes were red. She leaned in close and flapped her wings excitedly. *"Flea!"* she squawked.

Eew. Zeus pinched his nose between two fingers. Her breath reeked, and not in a good way. It smelled sort of like skunk mixed with stinky cheese. But where did she get off calling him a flea? Come on, he wasn't *that* small!

"Bick off, buds," he commanded. Not understanding him, the Harpies only cocked their heads curiously.

Zeus let go of his nose just long enough to repeat himself. "Back off, birds!" But they didn't back off, so he pinched his nose closed again.

Now all five birds began squawking at him. *"Flea! Flea!"* Bird breath surrounded him. Mega-stink!

"I'm not a flea! I'm a boy!" Zeus protested. Hearing the sound of footsteps and horses' hooves, he got to his feet. He peeked over the red-eyed Harpy's wing.

Beyond her a bunch of half-giants were swarming toward them! The birds' breathtakingly bad breath could probably knock them out at twenty paces. But whose side were these birds on? His or the half-giants'?

"Flea!" The red-eyed Harpy flapped her wings now as if shooing him away.

Zeus unpinched his nose again. "Oh, I get it! You mean *flee*? As in run? Good idea." He looked around. Behind him were steps leading up to some kind of temple. In front of him were smelly Harpies. And just beyond them were boy-eating half-giants.

He was no idiot, despite what the half-giants back on the ship had thought. "Thanks for the ride!" he told the birds. "Maybe I can do you a favor sometime." Seeing no better choice, he turned and dashed up the steps, taking them two at a time.

The Harpies lifted off, beating the half-giant attackers with their wings to delay them. Once he was inside the temple, Zeus looked for a way out the back.

The temple was round, but it wasn't very big. Its floor and walls were made of gleaming white marble stone. Tall columns stood all along its surrounding walls, and its roof was a dome. But there was no exit door.

Outside he heard shouts. Some of the Cronies

had managed to slip past the birds. Any minute now he'd be captured. He had to do something—and fast!

Zeus spied some small urns by one wall. But they weren't big enough for him to hide in. There was a low table standing right in the center of the floor. It was draped with a long dark blue tablecloth. And for some reason there was a big rock sitting on top of it. The rock was shaped like a cone and was about half as tall as he was.

Zeus dashed toward the table. He was hoping there was room enough for him to dive under it and hide.

Stomp! Stomp! Stomp! Too late! The soldiers were inside the temple now, almost upon him. Footsteps pounded closer. "There he is!" boomed a voice. "Get him!" called another.

Desperately, Zeus looked around for a weapon

to hold them off. Something. Anything! Seeing a long, jagged stick stuck point-first in the cone-shaped stone, he reached for it.

And pulled.

The jagged stick slid from the stone like a knife from a ripe peach. He'd been expecting it to be harder to get out. Now he stumbled backward under the force of his pull.

The bright white stick glowed in his hand. Its edges looked razor sharp, its blade highly polished. Only, it wasn't a stick at all, he realized. It was more like a sword. But not like any sword he'd every seen or heard about.

Swords were straight, not crooked like a zig-zag. And this thing was as long as he was tall. Yet it was lighter than the wooden sword he'd made back home.

Gripping it in both hands, he waved it at his attackers. It made a crackling, whooshing sound

with his every swing. He'd felt brave as he practiced with his homemade wooden sword earlier that morning. But this was a real fight. And now his hands shook.

The point of the zigzag sword struck the lead soldier's breastplate armor. Sparks flew. The half-giants stopped in their tracks.

Suddenly they were backing away, whispering in awe. "He pulled it out!" "Who is he?" "How could a mortal boy manage what no one else could do?"

Zeus stared in horror at what he held. Because he'd just noticed something really weird and kind of scary. The zigzag blade he'd pulled from the stone wasn't a stick. And it wasn't a sword, either.

No—instead, it was an actual, sparking, sizzling, terrifying *thunderbolt*!

CHAPTER SIX

The Woman in the Mist

WAIT TILL KING CRONUS HEARS ABOUT this!" shouted one of the Cronies. He ran from the temple and clomped down the front stairs. Then he leaped onto his horse and galloped away.

The remaining half-giant soldiers continued to back away from Zeus and his thunderbolt. Seeing how scared they all were, Zeus felt braver.

"Yeah, that's right," he taunted. "You *better*

run!" He lunged, brandishing the bolt like he'd practiced with his wooden sword back home.

Cowering, the half-giants fled from the temple and down the steps. But they didn't go any farther. So how was he going to escape with them waiting outside?

One thing was for sure: He was not going to take this thunderbolt with him when he got his chance to run. He glanced at it out of the corner of one eye, worried. What if it decided to turn on him, jumping out of his hand to strike him?

Bending low, he carefully laid it on the marble floor. Then he let go of it. Or tried to, anyway.

His fingers wouldn't open! Using his other hand, he tried to peel them away from the bolt. But his fingers only curled more tightly around it. Had the force of the electricity within it melded it to his skin? No, he didn't feel burned or anything.

Pzzzt! The jagged bolt suddenly glowed more brightly and crackled with electric sparks.

"Get off me!" Zeus shrieked in alarm. He shook his hand hard. No luck. This bolt was stuck to him like stink on a Harpy.

Hearing a hissing sound behind him, he jumped around. Abruptly a long crack split the polished marble floor just a few feet away from him. A great puff of golden, glittery steam escaped the crack. It formed a dazzling misty cloud as it rose into the air.

A woman's voice spoke from within the mist. "Are you the one?"

Zeus squinted into the big steam cloud. It popped and winked and fizzed. Was this what magic looked like? "Who's there? Are you talking to me?" he asked.

A woman stepped out of the mist cloud. Zeus couldn't help staring at her. Her shiny hair was black as midnight. Snowy white robes covered her from head to toe. All he could see was her face.

He couldn't see her eyes, though. Because the eyeglasses she wore were completely fogged from the glittery mist around her.

The woman's arm lifted slowly. She pointed a long finger at the thunderbolt. "Did you pull that from the stone?"

"Oh, sorry. Was it yours?" Zeus asked hopefully. "Because you can have it back. Here, take it." He held it out to her, disappointed when she didn't accept his offer.

She circled him. The cloud of mist followed her. "You are young, as in the prophecy," she said, studying him from all angles. "Yes, yes, I see," she said after a few moments. "It all makes sense now."

What made sense? Zeus wondered. And

how could she see anything at all through those foggy eyeglasses?

She put her fingertips to her forehead as if she were concentrating hard. He didn't have time for this, he thought impatiently. He had to escape those Cronies!

After setting the thunderbolt on the ground again, he stood on it this time. Then he yanked on his arm. *Rats.* He still couldn't get the bolt off.

"Your name!" the lady demanded, lowering her hands. "Is it Goose?"

"Goose? No! It's Zeus," he mumbled, embarrassed. He'd always thought his name was a little odd. Most kids in Crete were named Alexander or Nicholas or something equally cool and strong-sounding. But even the name Zeus was better than Goose!

"Ah, you must forgive me," the woman said.

As he straightened, she gave him a small bow. "I am Pythia, the oracle here at the Delphi temple. I can see the future, but sometimes my vision is blurred. Due to the mist, you understand?"

There was a loud hissing, and another cloud of steam shot up from the ground. The mist grew thicker around her.

Excitement rose in Zeus at her words. "If you can see the future, tell me this: How will I get this thunderbolt off me?"

She shook her head, her robe swaying back and forth. "That, I cannot see. For what is revealed is not mine to choose."

Zeus's stomach sank. What kind of crummy power was that?

As if she'd read his thoughts, or at least sensed his disappointment, Pythia added, "But one thing I do know: Your thunderbolt has amazing magic."

"Magic? Really?" Zeus stared at the bolt. It glowed, looking extra sparky, as if it were excited to have his attention. Interesting. He'd heard of magical things before, but he'd never seen one in action. He'd certainly never expected to *have* one. Had he been too quick to try to get rid of it?

"Only the trueborn king of the Olympians could have removed that bolt from the cone-stone," Pythia informed him.

King of the Olympians? Him? *This lady doesn't know what she's talking about,* thought Zeus.

He shook his head slowly. "No way," he told her. "I'm no king. I'm just a mortal kid. Maybe you should keep looking for that Goose guy. He's probably the one you want."

Although he couldn't see her eyes through those foggy specs, Zeus sensed her keen interest in him. A small silence passed, and then she said, "I have been too hasty. You are not yet ready to know all that has been prophesied. So for now let us simply call you a . . . a hero in training."

"A hero?" said Zeus. His face lit up. "Epic!" This was more like it, he thought. Heroes had cool adventures. They went on quests and did other manly stuff. "What is my quest? What important thing will you have me do?"

"Go where the cone-stone leads you," she answered.

What does that mean? Zeus wondered. Then he had a thought. Maybe this cone-stone would lead him to his parents!

But before he could ask about that, Pythia stepped backward into the mist again. "Never fear," her disembodied voice called out. "We will speak again . . . and soon."

"Wait!" Zeus leaped forward, dragging the thunderbolt after him. "I have more questions. Don't go yet!"

CHAPTER SEVEN

Mysterious Symbols

ZEUS RAN INTO THE MIST, SEARCHING for the oracle. But she was gone.

"What am I going to do now?" he wailed, staring at the thunderbolt. It was still dangling from his hand. "I can't walk around with this thing stuck to me for the rest of my life."

Go where the cone-stone leads you, Pythia had said. If the stone could *lead* him, it must be magic too. Like the thunderbolt. Could the magic stone help free him of this zappy, clingy bolt as well as find his parents? he wondered.

Going over to the table, Zeus walked all the way around it. He examined the cone-shaped stone atop it from all sides. There were strange black symbols on it that he hadn't noticed earlier. But he couldn't read them.

He *was* able to read the words that someone had scratched in the blank spaces between the symbols, though. He read them aloud: "Help us! We are in Cronus."

As the last word left his lips, there was a scraping sound. Then . . . *pop!* A chip of rock cracked away from the main cone-stone and fell to the ground.

It bounced across the temple floor toward the urns near the wall. Zeus went looking for the chip, dragging the bolt along with him. He was just about to give up on finding it when he heard a muffled squeak under his sandal heel. It sounded like a tiny voice!

He lifted his foot and saw the cone-stone chip lying there on the temple floor. It was oval-shaped. Zeus picked it up and studied it. It was gray and smooth, like the main stone. But it was only the size of his fist, with a small, round hole through one end. It also had some of those weird black symbols on it.

"Did you say something?" he asked it. A little embarrassed, he looked around, hoping no one had seen him talking to a rock. Luckily, he was alone inside the temple now. But he could still hear the half-giants hanging around outside on the steps, waiting for him.

When he looked back at the chip, his blue eyes widened. The symbols on it had moved around! Now they formed two words: *Find Poseidon.*

As the letters faded back into symbols again, goose bumps prickled Zeus's arms. He wasn't sure if Poseidon was a person, place, or thing, but he was excited all the same. Because he was pretty sure this cone-stone chip was sending him on a quest. Wow! Maybe he really was a hero in training!

"What and where is Poseidon?" he asked the chip. Maybe it was the name of the place where his parents were. Or maybe Poseidon was his father's name!

But no new words appeared on the chip's surface. It didn't speak, either. He asked it again. And again. But the chip wouldn't reply.

Annoyed, Zeus tossed it over his shoulder. It was just an ordinary piece of rock after all, he decided. Not magical.

"Ow-yip!" a tiny voice cried as the rock hit the floor.

Zeus rushed over to the rock and snatched it up again. "So you *did* speak."

"Uh-dip." It was almost like the chip of stone was rolling its eyes at him for being dense. But stones didn't have eyes. It was speaking some kind of foreign language he couldn't understand.

Pzzzt!

"Ow!" said Zeus. The jagged thunderbolt had shot sparks into his palm. They stung like tiny insect bites, but the pain swiftly faded.

Hmm, he thought. The chip of stone had said "ow-yip" a minute ago when he'd dropped it. Had it been saying "ow" too?

As if the bolt's sparks had sparked an idea, a light went on in his brain. He lifted the small gray rock closer. "Are you speaking Chip Latin?"

The rock stayed silent.

Maybe it hadn't understood him, thought Zeus. "Like Pig Latin," he explained. "Where you move the first letter of a word to the end of it and then add an 'ay' sound." He paused. "Only you're moving the first letter of a word to the end and adding an 'ip' sound instead. As in 'chip.' Right?"

"Ight-rip," said the chip.

Which must mean "right," Zeus decided.

Stomp! Stomp! Stomp! His eyes whipped toward the temple door. Someone was coming up the temple's front steps. Someone with big feet. Still clutching the chip, he dove under the table the cone-stone sat upon.

Luckily, the table turned out to be just tall enough for him to huddle under. He looked at the bolt. It was too big, poking out from under the tablecloth. Whoever was coming would surely see it and figure out his hiding place.

"Oh! Why can't you be *small*?" he moaned softly.

Suddenly the bolt made a crunching sound, like ice cracking on a winter pond. In an instant it shrank until it was no longer than a dagger!

The stomping crossed the temple floor toward him. The new arrivals surrounded the cone-stone. They stood so close that the toes of their sandals stuck under the tablecloth on all sides of Zeus. There were six feet in all, which meant three soldiers.

Zeus tucked himself tighter, scarcely daring to breathe. Clutching the bolt in one hand and the chip of stone in the other, he waited, trembling. Right now he didn't feel at all like a hero. Not even a hero in training!

CHAPTER EIGHT

The Big Bad Bully King

SO IT'S TRUE. THE MAGIC THUNDERBOLT is gone," Zeus heard a deep voice boom. It sounded familiar.

"Do you think that Snackboy really could have pulled it out like everyone's saying?"

Under the table, Zeus's eyes went wide. That sounded like Double Chin! And the first voice had been Lion Tattoo's. That storm must have blown their ship here extra, extra fast!

"Well, he's not here to ask. And we don't dare go back to King Cronus empty-handed," added a third voice. It was Blackbeard's.

Zeus felt the chip twitch in his palm. He looked down at it. The black symbols on it had rearranged themselves again. Now they spelled: *Danger.*

Well, that was helpful. Not! The chip hadn't told him anything he didn't *already* know. There was nowhere to run. He was surrounded.

"If there's magic in the thunderbolt, there may be magic in the cone-stone, too," Lion Tattoo mused. "King Cronus likes magic. Might toss us a coin or two for it. Let's take the stone to him."

Zeus heard a scraping noise overhead. And soon heavy footsteps thumped across the floor and left the temple.

"Young Zeus has escaped!" he heard Lion

Tattoo call to the crowd of half-giants outside. "Spread out and find him. A handsome reward will be given to he who delivers the boy to the king!"

A roar went up from the soldiers. There were more stomping sounds as they all began to leave.

Once it was quiet, Zeus crawled out from under the table. He wasn't surprised to see that the big cone-stone was gone.

He tiptoed across the temple floor. In the distance he could see Lion Tattoo and his two companions moving through the forest. They were knocking down olive trees and crushing grapevines along the way. All the other half-giants were gone too. They were searching for him when he was right here under their big noses. Ha!

Hmm. Lion Tattoo was carrying the cone-stone under one arm. Oracle Pythia had

instructed him to go where the stone led. Well then, he supposed he'd better follow!

Zeus had only taken a single step toward the door when suddenly Lion Tattoo turned and looked back toward the temple. Zeus dove behind a column, his heart hammering in his chest. Had he been seen? But when he dared to check again, none of his enemies were looking his way.

He needed to get going, before the trio of half-giants got too far ahead of him. But what if he got caught following them and was taken before the king?

Zeus hesitated, still safe behind the column. King Cronus was not a nice guy. First of all, he was a Titan. Rumor had it that Titan giants were *twice* as mean as half-giants. And Cronus was the biggest, baddest Titan of them all!

And Poseidon might actually have nothing

whatsoever to do with his parents. If so, why should he rescue this Poseidon—whoever or whatever he was? "For all I know, Poseidon could be the name of another dumb thunderbolt," he grumbled.

"Ow!" he yelled as the bolt zapped him again. "Stop that!" This annoying thunderbolt was the cause of all his problems. It had doomed him to accept responsibilities he'd neither wanted nor asked for. Now the stone chip twitched in his palm again. It was like the chip and the bolt were both ganging up on him! He glanced down at the chip. The symbols on it had reshaped to form a new word: *Follow*.

Still Zeus hesitated. Maybe it would be smarter to hightail it back to Crete. There he could be safe and cozy again in his cave. But was that really what he wanted?

His feet began to move. Almost like they had

decided to obey the bolt and the chip on their own. Before he knew it, he was dashing down the steps. He paused at the bottom.

"Okay, feet. You win." Pulling the leather string tie from the neck of his tunic, he threaded it through the hole in the pesky chip. Then he tied the two ends of the string together so it formed a loop.

He slipped it over his head so the chip hung around his neck like an amulet. Which wasn't exactly easy to do with a thunderbolt stuck to his hand!

Immediately the chip amulet began to twitch against his chest. "Something on your mind, Chip?" Zeus asked it.

"Ing-kip an-cip ree-fip olt-bip," the stone chip informed him.

"King can free bolt," Zeus translated. Excitement filled him as he realized what that must mean. That the king knew how to make the bolt let go of him.

On the one hand, Cronus was a terrible bully. There was no telling what the king might do to him. But on the other hand, he didn't have much choice about what to do now. Because on his other hand there was a thunderbolt!

Zeus couldn't imagine going through the rest of his life—however long that might be—with a thunderbolt stuck to him. He wanted it gone!

"Well, that settles it, then." Picking up his pace, Zeus was soon hot on the trail of Lion Tattoo and his two half-giant pals.

CHAPTER NINE

Gulp!

IT WAS ALMOST NIGHTFALL BY THE TIME Zeus reached the king's camp. Staying hidden behind a tree, he counted six Titan giants seated around a blazing fire. They were gobbling dinner and making plans. War plans, from the sound of it.

"Under my iron fist, Earth is now right where I want it. In terrible turmoil," one of them was saying. He wore a golden crown and had an evil gleam in his eye. This had to be King Cronus himself! Especially since the cone-stone sat right beside him on the ground.

It was hard to hear the giants over the sound of their munching, slurping, and crunching. Zeus sneaked closer. As he watched, the king pulled something from his mouth. Then he tossed whatever it was onto a huge pile behind him. A pile of mortal bones!

The king rubbed his hands together in glee. "Soon we will unleash the Creatures of Chaos in each of our realms. Mortals will be quaking in their sandals like never before! Heh-heh-heh!"

No kidding, thought Zeus. In fact, his knees were already knocking, just hearing about the creatures. Weren't any of the other Titans going to stop this rotten king from putting his dastardly plans into action?

"What about the Olympians?" one of them dared to ask. His entire head glowed sort of like a pale sun. "You've failed to capture them all." The others nodded, grumbling.

King Cronus slammed a meaty fist on his knee, looking fierce. "I've captured five." For some reason, he rubbed his belly as he said this. He had the most enormous belly Zeus had ever seen. It stuck out so far over his belt that it almost covered his thighs.

"But more are still on the loose—a threat to us," another Titan argued. This one had a large pair of wings sticking out behind him. "We've heard rumors there could be as many as a dozen all together."

"If there are more, I will find them all and jail them," Cronus began.

"In your belly? No, I think it would be safer to jail them separately," the Sunhead Titan insisted. "At the far corners of the Earth. And under guard!"

Zeus gasped. So that's why Cronus's belly was so big! It was full of Olympians, whoever they were. *Yuck!*

Wait a minute! The message scratched on the cone-stone had said: *We are in Cronus!* The Olympians must've written it somehow. And Pythia had said that the king of the Olympians was supposed to pull the thunderbolt from the cone-stone. Only *Zeus* had done it instead.

What if Poseidon was the true Olympian king instead of that Goose guy? That made sense, didn't it? Why else would Chip be so anxious for Zeus to find him? Hey! If Poseidon was inside Cronus and Zeus got him out, maybe Poseidon would take this thunderbolt off his hands—um, hand.

As if it could read his mind, the thunderbolt

gave a hard jolt. Zeus heard that ice-crunching sound again. "No! Not now, Bolt!" he hissed.

But in an instant the bolt flashed to its full length. It sparked and sizzled with electricity. Unfortunately, as it expanded, it accidentally sliced through the trunk of the tree Zeus was hiding behind. It crashed to the ground, barely missing him.

The twelve giants' heads whipped around to stare in his direction.

"Who's there?" demanded Cronus, leaping to his feet. Standing tall, he looked even more terrifying than he had while seated.

"Small! Small!" Zeus hissed urgently. At his command the bolt shrank again. He wasn't quite ready to meet the king after all, he decided. He whirled around to run.

But before he could take a step, something poked through the back of his tunic. "Gotcha,

Snackboy!" He was yanked upward on the tip of a spear. Lion Tattoo's spear. Double Chin and Blackbeard stood beside him, grinning.

Zeus had been so busy spying, he hadn't noticed the half-giants sneaking up on him. As he dangled in midair, the half-giants carried him over to the Titans sitting around the fire.

He felt the chip amulet shudder against his chest. Quickly he tucked it inside the neck of his tunic, where it couldn't be seen.

"We have found Zeus, Your Majesty!" Lion Tattoo announced, bowing on one knee. Lowering the angle of the spear, he dropped Zeus before the king. The half-giants looked at the king expectantly, obviously hoping for a reward. They frowned mightily when Cronus merely waved them away.

Meanwhile, Zeus had landed on all fours at Cronus's feet. The Titans closed in around him.

Suddenly it began to snow. *Huh? It's not winter,* thought Zeus. And why was it snowing around him but nowhere else?

He tasted one of the snowflakes. Salt! Looking up, he saw the king's giant hand hovering above him. He was pouring salt out of a glass shaker. Onto *him.*

As far as Zeus knew, the only things that got salted were slugs and dinner. He wasn't a slug. Which meant Cronus must be planning to make him—*Yikes!*

"Why does everyone want to eat me today?" Zeus complained.

Peering down at him over his great big belly, Cronus laughed. "Heh-heh-heh! This one's funny."

Zeus leaped to his feet, brushing salt from his hair. "Release Poseidon!" he demanded.

The king laughed even harder, slapping his knee. "Yeah, right! You are one hilarious kid.

It's gonna be fun having you around for an eternity." Plucking Zeus up by the back of his tunic, he lifted him high overhead.

Cronus tilted his head back. "Over the teeth and past the gums, look out, belly, here Zeus comes!" His giant mouth opened wide.

From somewhere down below, Zeus heard voices. They sounded like they were coming from deep in a cave. Or from inside Cronus's belly!

"Let us out! Help! Can you hear us?"

The Olympians! Was Poseidon among them? If he could somehow make the bolt let go, and if he could somehow trick Cronus into swallowing it, maybe Poseidon would catch it and fight his way out. Then the thunderbolt could be *his* problem instead of Zeus's.

Without warning, Cronus's fingers released him. Zeus fell feetfirst straight toward a gaping black pit full of teeth. *Nooo!* He wanted Cronus to swallow the bolt, not swallow him!

In the nick of time Zeus spread his legs. He landed with his feet braced on either side of Cronus's nose. A big tongue swiped around, reaching for him. *It's now or never,* he thought desperately.

Drawing back one arm, Zeus yelled, "Fly!" He hurled the bolt down the Titan giant's throat. Then he looked down at his hand, hardly able to believe it. The thunderbolt had obeyed him. It was gone!

The giant's eyes widened. His mouth snapped shut as if he'd accidentally swallowed a bug. A *lightning* bug! His face turned red, and he wrapped his hands around his own throat. He swayed, like a giant oak tree in a storm.

Zeus lost his footing and tumbled backward. He began to fall. Catching a button on the front of Cronus's tunic, he hung on for dear life.

"Wait! I know what to do!" Sunhead ran to

stand behind Cronus. He wrapped his beefy arms around his chest, just above the spot where Zeus was hanging. Sunhead linked his fists over the king's solar plexus. Then he pulled, hard.

King Cronus turned a sickly green. And then suddenly . . . *BLEAEAH!* He barfed! Big time.

A huge stream of ookiness blasted out of his mouth like water from a fountain. Only it wasn't water. It was gross stuff. The force of it slammed into Zeus, knocking him toward the ground. He slid down Cronus's belly like it was a vomit slide.

Sploosh! Zeus fell into the big barf swamp that was forming at the king's feet. It was a swirling mess of epic proportions. There were beast bones, unidentifiable gloppy goo, and five lumps. The lumps were each about the same size as Zeus. And they were moving!

Zeus stood up. Or tried to. He kept sliding and landing on his butt again.

"Eew!" a voice shrieked. "This is disgusting!" It was a girl. She was slipping and sliding too. Despite the goo that covered her, Zeus could see that her long hair was golden. And her eyes were as blue as his own.

Meanwhile, Cronus was moaning and holding his stomach. Seeming to all of a sudden figure out what had happened, he managed to yell, "Get them!"

Then things happened fast. The Titan giants began grabbing up the lumps. One giant snatched up the cone-stone, too.

Zeus tried to get to his feet. He had to fight the giants off! But just as one of them reached for him, Zeus was swept downhill. Carried off on a whooshing river of yuck. At the bottom of the hill he slammed into a rock.

Instantly everything went dark, and he knew no more.

CHAPTER TEN

Olympians

"P.U. SOMETHING STINKS!" ZEUS SAID woozily.

"It's you," said a girl's voice. "I've already bathed in the waterfall."

Zeus remembered that voice. The girl with the long golden hair!

Suddenly everything came back to him. He leaped to his feet, looking around for the Titans. It was morning. He was at the bottom of a hill, surrounded by enormous boulders and trees. He'd slid a long way from where the Titans had built their fire. King Cronus and the others were nowhere in sight.

He sniffed himself. The stink was definitely him. *Ugh.* At least he was finally free of the thunderbolt. He looked around again, making sure it wasn't sneaking up on him or anything. Was it still in Cronus's belly, or—

"So he's finally awake?" asked a boy's voice.

Zeus turned his head to see a boy with turquoise eyes coming toward them. The girl and the boy were both about his age, as far as he could tell. "You wouldn't be Poseidon by any chance?" Zeus asked the boy.

"Who wants to know?" asked the girl.

But the boy nodded at the same time. "Yeah, I am. And she's Hera."

"Yes!" said Zeus, pumping a fist. Despite all

that had gone wrong, he'd managed to succeed in his first quest. He'd followed the cone-stone and found Poseidon. Turned out Poseidon was a kid, not his dad. It was disappointing, but finding his parents would just have to wait.

"What's your name?" Hera demanded.

"Zeus."

Hera and Poseidon gave each other a startled look. "Isn't that the name Cronus called out before he swallowed the cone-st—" Poseidon started to say. Hera elbowed him before he could finish.

"Swallowed what?" Zeus asked.

Hera put on a fake kind of smile. "Oh, nothing. How did you find us, anyway?"

"I was sent here to rescue you. By an oracle. And by *this*." Zeus lifted the chip amulet that hung around his neck.

Poseidon stepped closer to examine it, then fanned his face. "Maybe you should take a shower before we talk." He pointed toward the waterfall beyond some trees nearby.

Quickly Zeus went to bathe in the waterfall and wash his tunic. Afterward he put his wet tunic and sandals back on.

When he returned to his companions, he explained everything. He told them all that had happened to him since leaving Crete. Including how Pythia had called him a hero in training.

"Well, she sure got that wrong," Hera scoffed.

"Gosh, don't try to spare my feelings or anything," said Zeus.

"No, I just meant—" She glanced at Poseidon. "Think we can trust him?"

Poseidon shrugged. "Your call."

Hera studied Zeus intently, then shook her head. "No, I don't think we'll trust you quite yet. You could be one of Cronus's spies."

"I'm not!" Zeus insisted.

"You can prove it to us, then," she said.

"How?"

"There were three more of us imprisoned in Cronus's belly," Hera told him. "Hestia, Demeter, and Hades. We escaped, but the Titan giants made off with the others. If you help us rescue them, we'll tell you a secret. A big one."

They'd been captive in a belly for ten years. What kind of secrets could they know? wondered Zeus. "King Cronus said you're Olympians. What's that?" he asked.

"We don't actually know," Poseidon replied.

"But it's something the king is afraid of," added Hera. "So that must mean we have some kind of magic powers."

"If only we knew how to use them!" said Poseidon.

With a loud rumble, the ground next to them

suddenly split open. Zeus, Hera, and Poseidon jumped back. A cloud of glittery mist appeared. Pythia's face glowed within it.

"It's her! It's the oracle I told you about!" Zeus exclaimed.

"Trouble, trouble, boil, and bubble!" the oracle murmured. "You must find the trident. One that will point the way to those you seek. One that—in the right hands—has the power to defeat the first of the king's Creatures of Chaos."

As quickly as the mist appeared, it disappeared again.

"Huh? Which hands are the right hands?" asked Poseidon.

"Probably mine," Zeus and Hera said at the same time.

Zeus rolled his eyes. He'd grown up around girls. But the nymph, the bee, and the goat who'd raised him had always let him have his way. He had a feeling this girl was going to be different.

"Come on, let's get going," Poseidon said. "See that hill over there? Maybe if we climb to the top, we can figure out which way to go."

"So we're supposed to find a trident," said Zeus as they started to walk. "Shouldn't be too hard."

Hera and Poseidon nodded. The three continued on for a bit without saying anything more. Finally Zeus said, "One question. What's a trident?"

Hera and Poseidon both shrugged. "No idea," they admitted at the same time.

"Well, I do know that 'tri' means 'three,'" said Hera.

"Like us?" said Poseidon. "There are three of us."

It wasn't much of a clue. Zeus frowned. How

were they going to find the trident when they didn't even know what it was? An hour later they reached the top of the hill.

Hera gasped. "Look!" On the distant horizon they saw land's end. Beyond it the entire sea was boiling.

Zeus felt his skin prickle. He repeated the oracle's words. "Trouble, trouble, boil, and bubble." Then he added, "I have a feeling that's where we'll find the trident. Our journey could be dangerous, though. Are we up for this?"

Hera lifted her chin. "Of course."

Poseidon nodded, but he looked a little nervous. "I hope the trident's not in that sea. I don't know how to swim."

Overhead the clouds darkened suddenly. The air crackled. *Uh-oh!* Zeus knew what that meant. But before he could warn his new friends—

Ka-pow!

The thunderbolt was back! It stood before him, crackling and sparking. He started to run downhill trying to get away from it. The bolt chased him.

"Small!" Zeus commanded, breathlessly coming to a stop at the bottom of the hill. In a flash the thunderbolt shrank to the size of a dagger. It hovered in the air before him, darting around as if wanting to be held. Zeus thrust his hands under his armpits so that the bolt couldn't get to them.

It buzzed around him, looking for a way in. Finally seeming to give up, it slid under the belt at the waist of his tunic. At least it hadn't managed to get stuck to his hand again.

"Good Bolt," said Zeus as Hera and Poseidon caught up to him. "Stay."

Poseidon's eyebrows went up in awe. "You have a thunderbolt for a pet?"

"Seems like it," said Zeus. "C'mon. Let's get going."

Hera rolled her eyes. "Who made you boss, Thunderboy?"

"Thunderboy?" Zeus echoed. He liked the sound of that.

Beyond the hill, he could feel the sea calling to him. Could feel his destiny beckon.

"Follow me," he said more firmly. And to his surprise, they did. With long, confident strides, he led the others toward the boiling sea.

Joan Holub is the award-winning author of more than one hundred and thirty books for young readers, including *Zero the Hero*, *Vincent van Gogh: Sunflowers and Swirly Stars*, and *Shampoodle*. She lives in North Carolina. Visit her at joanholub.com.

Suzanne Williams is the award-winning author of more than thirty-five books for young readers, including *Library Lil*, *Ten Naughty Little Monkeys*, and the Princess Power and Fairy Blossoms series. She lives near Seattle in Washington State. Visit her at suzanne-williams.com.